BELLA THE FLUTTERBY BUTTERFLY

Written by
Tiffany Berry

Illustrated by
Kristin Powell

Text Copyright© 2021 by Tiffany Berry

Illustration Copyright© 2021 by Kristin Powell

Published by Evergreen Press TX, LLC in 2021.

All rights reserved. No portion of this book may be reproduced, stored in a retrieval system, or transmitted in any form or by any means - electronic, mechanical, photocopy, recording, scanning, or other - except for brief quotations in critical reviews or articles, without the prior written permission of the publisher.

ISBN: 978-0-578-95636-7

Summary: A butterfly discovers that she is beautifully and wonderfully made by befriending a wise ladybug - provided by publisher.

www.evergreenpresstx.com

To our beautiful girls.
May you know God's love and ours.

"I praise you because I am fearfully and wonderfully made." Psalm 139:14

"Good morning, garden," said Bella, as she widened her brand-new wings. "It's time for some sunrise stretches so we can do our things."

"There are lots of friends to meet and greet;
I can't wait to say hello.
And all the flowers, fruits, and trees —
there are so many places to go!"

Just then some new friends fluttered by,
and Bella shined her biggest smile.
But they didn't stop. They didn't pause.
They zoomed past in a hurried style.

Bella widened her wings and flittered
as fast as she could go.
But she couldn't catch the others;
Bella's wings were much too slow.

So Bella found a spot to land
and hung her little head.
Just then she spotted something bright;
in fact, it was bright red.

"Hi, my name is Lulu the Ladybug.
It's nice to meet you, dear!
You look so sad. I want to help.
I'm glad you landed here!"

"It's nice to meet you, Lulu.
My name is Bella the Butterfly.
I'm having a hard day
watching others flutter by."

"I'm sorry you're sad, my friend,"
said Lulu. "I want to make you smile.
Let's talk about this garden;
come sit with me a while."

"You see this flower that I'm on, the color and the look? It's so unique and beautiful. It's special in my book."

"This flower is a lot like you;
it stands out among the crowd.
Each morning it looks up and smiles
because it is so proud."

"God chose it for this garden,
and He loves how it's displayed.
He feels the same about you;
you are beautifully and wonderfully made."

Bella's eyes opened wide and saw flowers
of red, blue, yellow, and pink.
Then she smiled, spread her wings,
and gave Lulu a big wink.

"*Thank you, Lulu,*" said Bella,
"*for helping me change my mind.
You taught me about joy
and that I am uniquely designed.*"

Bella saw the other butterflies
and headed straight their way.
She fluttered up right next to them
and asked if they would play.

They smiled at Bella and welcomed her
to join their garden crew.
It was full of insects big, small, bold, and
bright — there were more than just a few!

They said to Bella, *"We love your pretty wings.
It's neat to watch you fly!
When you fluttered over here,
the colors caught our eye."*

Bella smiled and said, *"Thank you,"*
to her new special friends.
And they fluttered together in the garden
until the sunset's end.

Each one of them is beautiful and makes the garden complete. YOU are beautiful just like this; now name one thing about you that's *UNIQUE!*

The Berry Family
(left to right) **Kira, Chris, London, and Tiffany**

This book started as a small God whisper in 2019. After watching the Lord bring this to life, it is certain that He has a message for all of us — we are uniquely and beautifully created in God's image.

Tiffany Berry and her husband, Chris, adopted their first daughter, Kira, in 2010. Watching Kira navigate the challenges she faces everyday (cerebral palsy, fetal alcohol syndrome, and OCD) has been one of the most beautiful gifts to the Berry family. It is her boldness and grit that inspired *Bella the Flutterby Butterfly*.

As kids would ride their bikes in the neighborhood, Kira would watch from her wheelchair. She would then fiercely move her chair as fast as she could to catch up with them. In one way, this broke her parents' hearts. In another, they were so proud of her tenacity!

In 2014, Kira's sister, London, was born. She is the inspiration for Lulu the Ladybug. Tiffany and Chris have affectionately called her "Londy Lulu" since birth. Between London's joy and Kira's tenacity, the Berry girls are a force to be reckoned with.

Tiffany and Chris long to transform these life lessons into teachable storybook moments for children. In 2021, Tiffany collaborated with her longtime friend and illustrator, Kristin Powell, to bring this book to life.

Made in the USA
Coppell, TX
11 August 2021